by Chris Kreie

illustrated by Marcus Smith

Librarian Reviewer
Katharine Kan
Graphic novel reviewer and Library Consultant, Panama City, FL
MLS in Library and Information Studies, University of Hawaii at Manoa, HI

Reading Consultant
Elizabeth Stedem
Educator/Consultant, Colorado Springs, CO
MA in Elementary Education, University of Denver, CO

Graphic Quest is published by Stone Arch Books
151 Good Counsel Drive, P.O. Box 669
Mankato, Minnesota 56002
www.stonearchbooks.com

Library of Congress Cataloging-in-Publication Data
Kreie, Chris.
Lost: A Tale of Survival / by Chris Kreie; illustrated by Marcus Smith.
p. cm. — (Graphic Quest)
ISBN-13: 978-1-59889-828-6 (library binding)
ISBN-10: 1-59889-828-0 (library binding)
ISBN-13: 978-1-59889-884-2 (paperback)
ISBN-10: 1-59889-884-1 (paperback)
1. Graphic novels. I. Smith, Marcus. II. Title.
PN6727.K69L67 2008
741.5'973—dc22 2007006245

Summary: Every summer, Eric and his dad go camping in northern Minnesota. This year, Eric brought his friend, and the boys explore the wilderness on their own. When Cris is injured, Eric must find the camp and save his friend.

Art Director: Heather Kindseth
Graphic Designer: Brann Garvey

1 2 3 4 5 6 12 11 10 09 08 07

Printed in the United States of America

TABLE OF CONTENTS

CHAPTER ONE

Every summer for the past five years, Eric Richardson and his dad had taken a trip to the Boundary Waters Canoe Area in northern Minnesota. This year they made the trip with their friends, the Russells. This was also the first year Eric's dad had let him bring a friend. Eric and Cris got to pilot a canoe together. They got to share a tent. And today, they were going to explore on their own. Cris was hoping to see a moose.

These lakes are nothing to mess with, guys. The water here in the river is cold, but the water out in the middle of a big lake is bone chilling. It could kill you.
Come on, Dad, we'll be fine. We'll be careful. Right, Cris?
No fooling around. Promise.

We know, Dad. Respect the water.
See you later, Mr. R!
It better not be too much later. You guys be back before dark.

The lake was fun to canoe in, but there wasn't much to see. In a few places, rivers split off from the lake. These seemed much more interesting to the boys.
Okay, I think if we head down the Moose River, over there it might be fun.
Cool, let's go!
Keep a look out for rocks, okay?
Okay.
But there were too many rocks. The boys couldn't steer around all of them.
CLUNK!
Whoa!

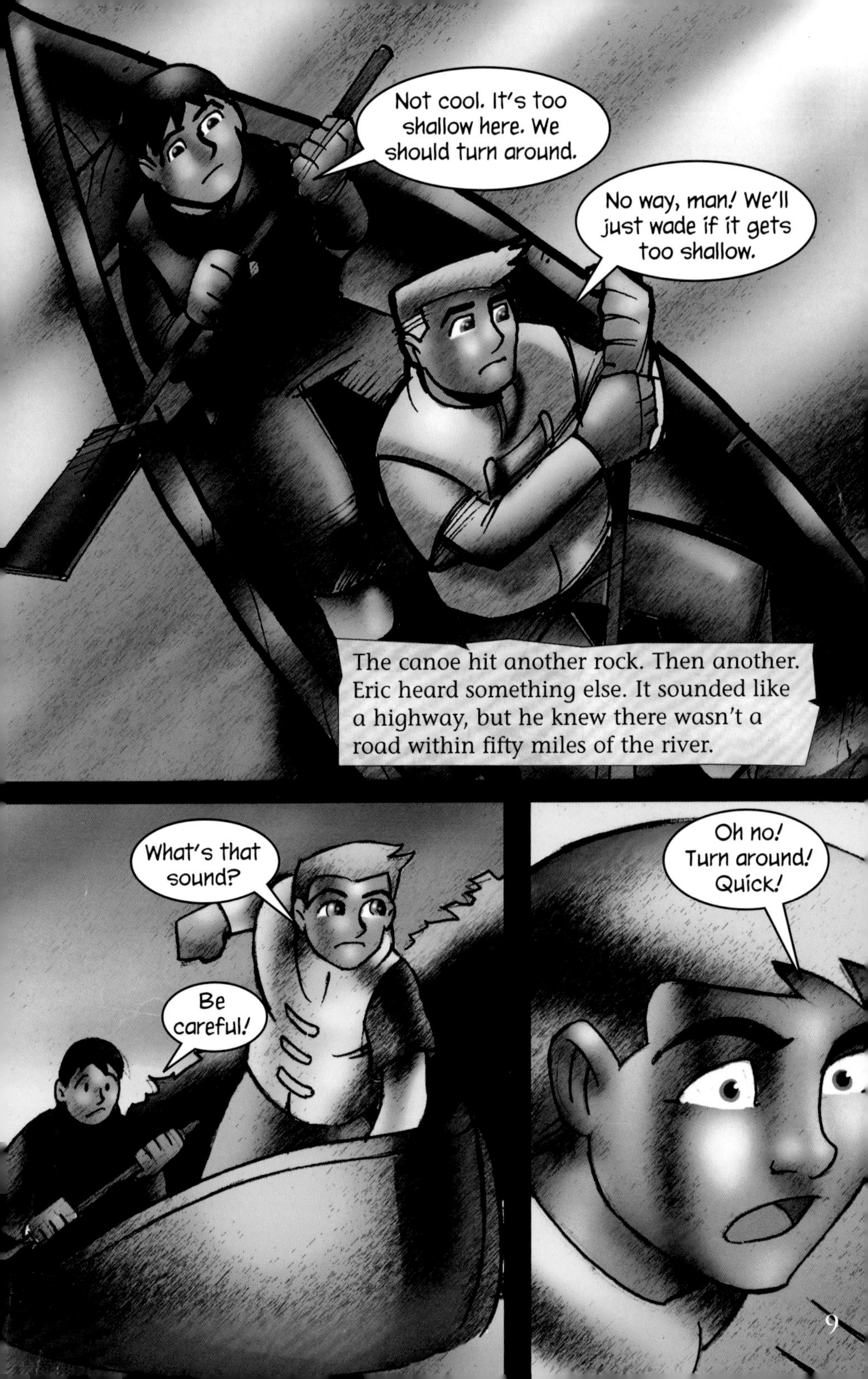

Not cool. It's too shallow here. We should turn around.

No way, man! We'll just wade if it gets too shallow.

The canoe hit another rock. Then another. Eric heard something else. It sounded like a highway, but he knew there wasn't a road within fifty miles of the river.

We've gotta get this canoe upstream right away. Huge rapids are ahead of us. We'll never make it down in one piece.
Cris paddled hard on his right side while Eric dug in on the left.
I don't think we can do it, Eric.
Yes we can! Shoot for the shoreline. If we make it there, we'll be fine.
The shoreline was still far away, and the water was moving fast. It was going to take all their strength to make it. Then the horrifying reality hit Eric.

We're going to shoot the rapids! We'll have to keep a look out for the big boulders.
Okay. We can do it!
Let's go!
It took muscles to steer the canoe over the rapids.
Right!
Left!
Okay, what's next?
I don't know.

Then suddenly, the river seemed to drop out from beneath them!
A waterfall!
Hold on, Cris!

AAGGHHH!

CHAPTER TWO

Eric knew it was pointless to try to fight the current or stop the canoe. The canoe bounced over a few smaller rocks and then veered toward the shore. Steering with all his might, Eric aimed the canoe for dry land.

Cris! Where are you?
His muscles ached from the effort, and the canoe began to slip out of his control.
Suddenly, the canoe hit a rock and flipped over.
Eric's dad had been right. The water was bone chilling.
Eric's heart was racing. He couldn't believe that their fun day canoeing had turned into this. It was like a bad dream.
I've got to find Cris! The water could kill him.
Eric stripped off his life jacket and rushed to find Cris.

Cris!
Cris, can you hear me?
A sharp pain in his foot forced him to stop.
When Eric looked down, he could see that the bottom of his foot was bleeding.
His foot must have gotten scraped on rocks in the river.
Thinking fast, Eric ripped a strip of fabric from his shirt and tied it around the wound.

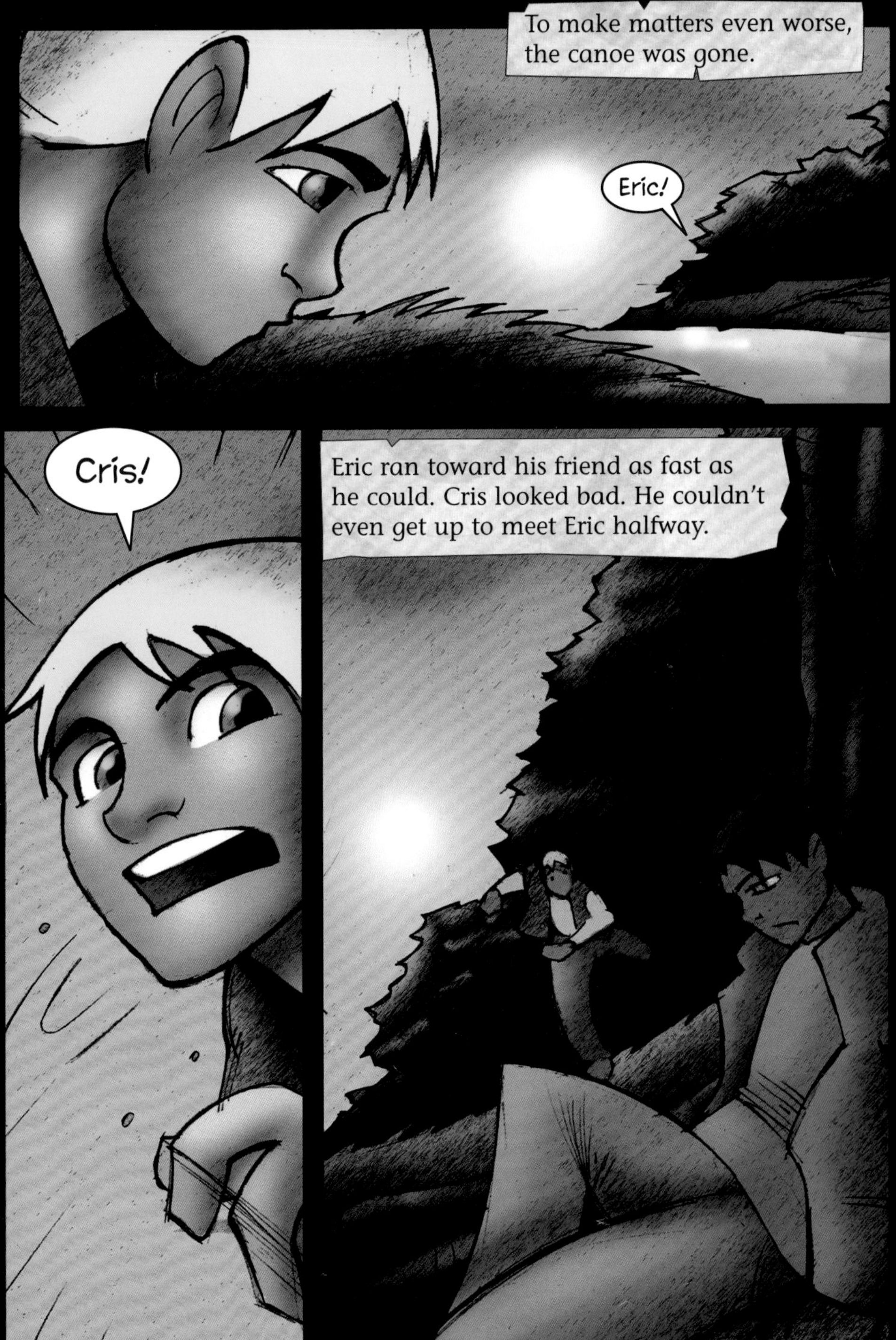

Eric ran toward his friend as fast as he could. Cris looked bad. He couldn't even get up to meet Eric halfway.

I can't believe you flew out of the canoe like that.
Are you okay?
I'm okay. But I'm pretty sure my ankle is broken.
My medicine is back at camp.
Cris was diabetic, which meant he had to give himself shots of insulin three times a day.

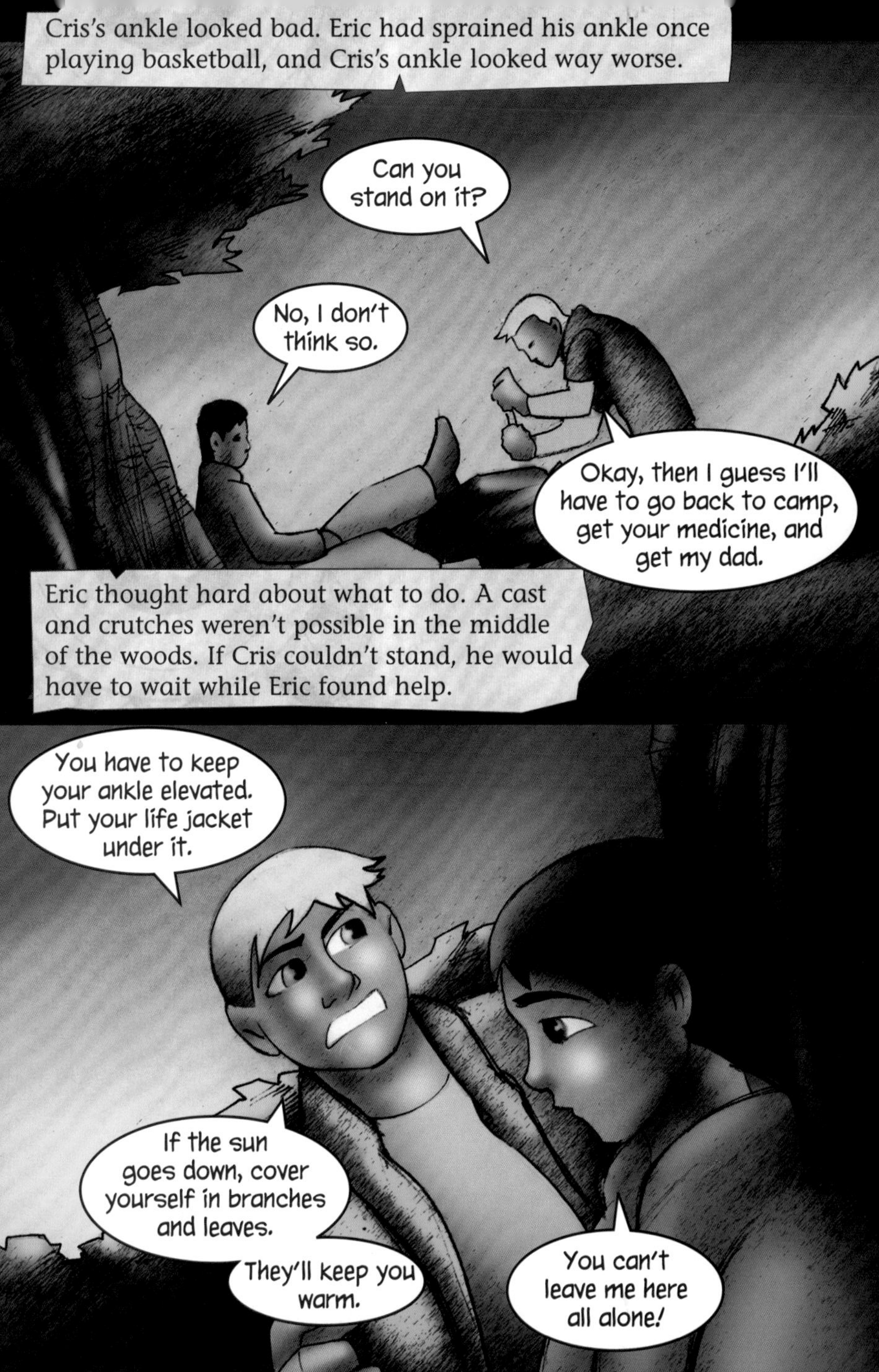
Cris's ankle looked bad. Eric had sprained his ankle once playing basketball, and Cris's ankle looked way worse.
Can you stand on it?
No, I don't think so.
Okay, then I guess I'll have to go back to camp, get your medicine, and get my dad.
Eric thought hard about what to do. A cast and crutches weren't possible in the middle of the woods. If Cris couldn't stand, he would have to wait while Eric found help.
You have to keep your ankle elevated. Put your life jacket under it.
If the sun goes down, cover yourself in branches and leaves.
They'll keep you warm.
You can't leave me here all alone!

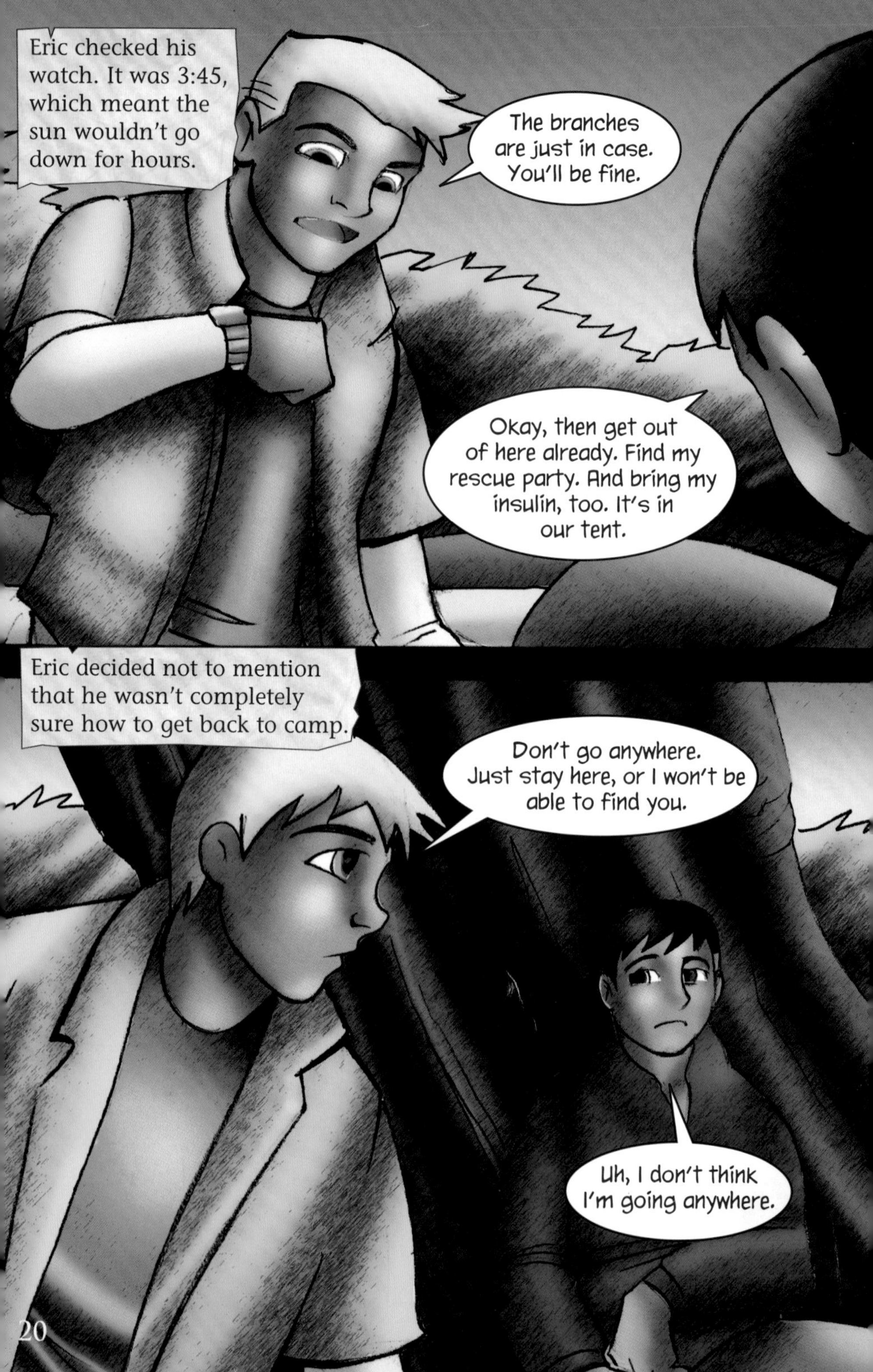
Eric checked his watch. It was 3:45, which meant the sun wouldn't go down for hours.
The branches are just in case. You'll be fine.
Okay, then get out of here already. Find my rescue party. And bring my insulin, too. It's in our tent.
Eric decided not to mention that he wasn't completely sure how to get back to camp.
Don't go anywhere. Just stay here, or I won't be able to find you.
Uh, I don't think I'm going anywhere.

I'll be back.
Eric didn't want to leave his friend all alone in the woods, but what else could he do?
Still feeling the pain on the bottom of his cut foot, Eric took off into the woods.
I guess I'll just . . . wait here.

Eric ran on a path alongside the river. Tall green trees shot into the sky all around him. The river looked different from here. It wasn't the scary beast that tossed Cris from the canoe. It was beautiful. When you sat next to the water, Eric thought, it seemed calm and peaceful. But when you were in it, the water made you fight for your life.
Above Eric, a bird cried out a lonely call.
That sounds like an osprey. Too bad I can't get a view from things up there.

Eric spread his map out on a rock. He moved his finger along the map until he saw the Moose River.
There's the river I'm on. Now, how do I get back to camp?
If he went straight west for a mile, he should be back at camp.
Eric knew what he had to do. He checked his compass and headed west into the forest.
Meanwhile . . .
I hope Eric gets back with my insulin fast.
Don't get lost, buddy. I'm counting on you.

CHAPTER THREE

Meanwhile . . .

Eric could see a valley below him. And just past that, a lake. According to the map, he should pass a portage trail before he got to the lake their camp was on.

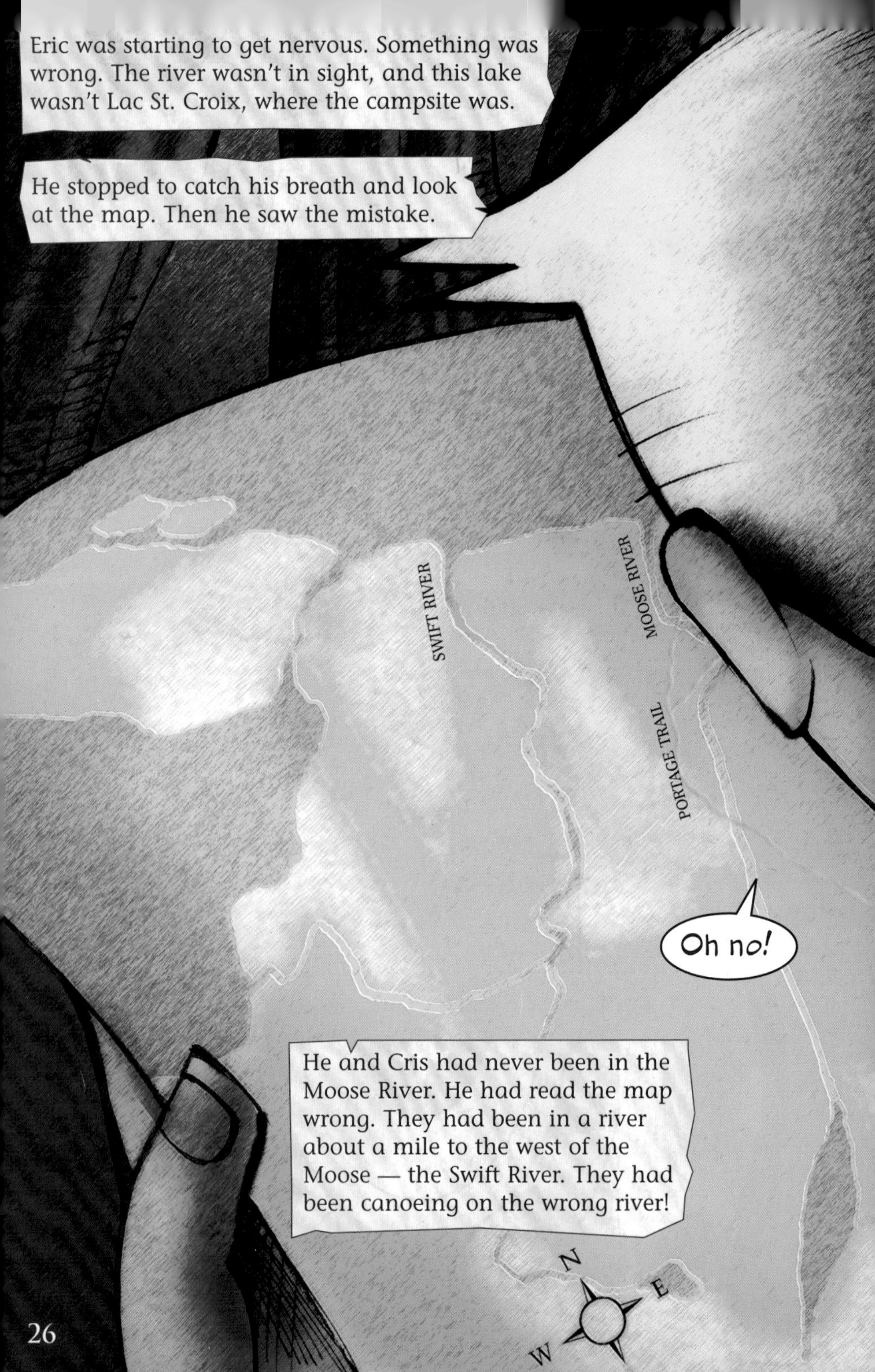
Eric was starting to get nervous. Something was wrong. The river wasn't in sight, and this lake wasn't Lac St. Croix, where the campsite was.
He stopped to catch his breath and look at the map. Then he saw the mistake.
SWIFT RIVER
MOOSE RIVER
PORTAGE TRAIL
Oh no!
He and Cris had never been in the Moose River. He had read the map wrong. They had been in a river about a mile to the west of the Moose — the Swift River. They had been canoeing on the wrong river!
N
E
W

Meanwhile . . .
Cris tried to keep himself in good spirits, but the going was rough and he wasn't even sure he was headed toward the campsite.
A quick rest should make me feel better.

That bird is huge! Eric would know what kind it is. Lucky for me, Eric's been in these woods before. He'll know how to get back to camp . . . I hope.

Using a branch as a crutch, Cris stood up.

Well, staying here isn't helping.

I should be able to do this.

Cris hit the ground hard. His strength was slipping away. He might have laid there longer if the mosquitoes weren't so bad.
BUZZ
BUZZ
Cris slowly tried to get to his feet. He was so dizzy he couldn't stand.

Cris wasn't just dizzy. He needed his medicine. And he needed to eat. It was a matter of life or death. He would have to find his way back to camp, no matter what.
Okay. I can do this.
Trying to ignore the sick feeling washing over him and the pain in his ankle, Cris slowly began to crawl along the river.
All I have to do is stay positive.
I can do this. I can make it.

CHAPTER FOUR

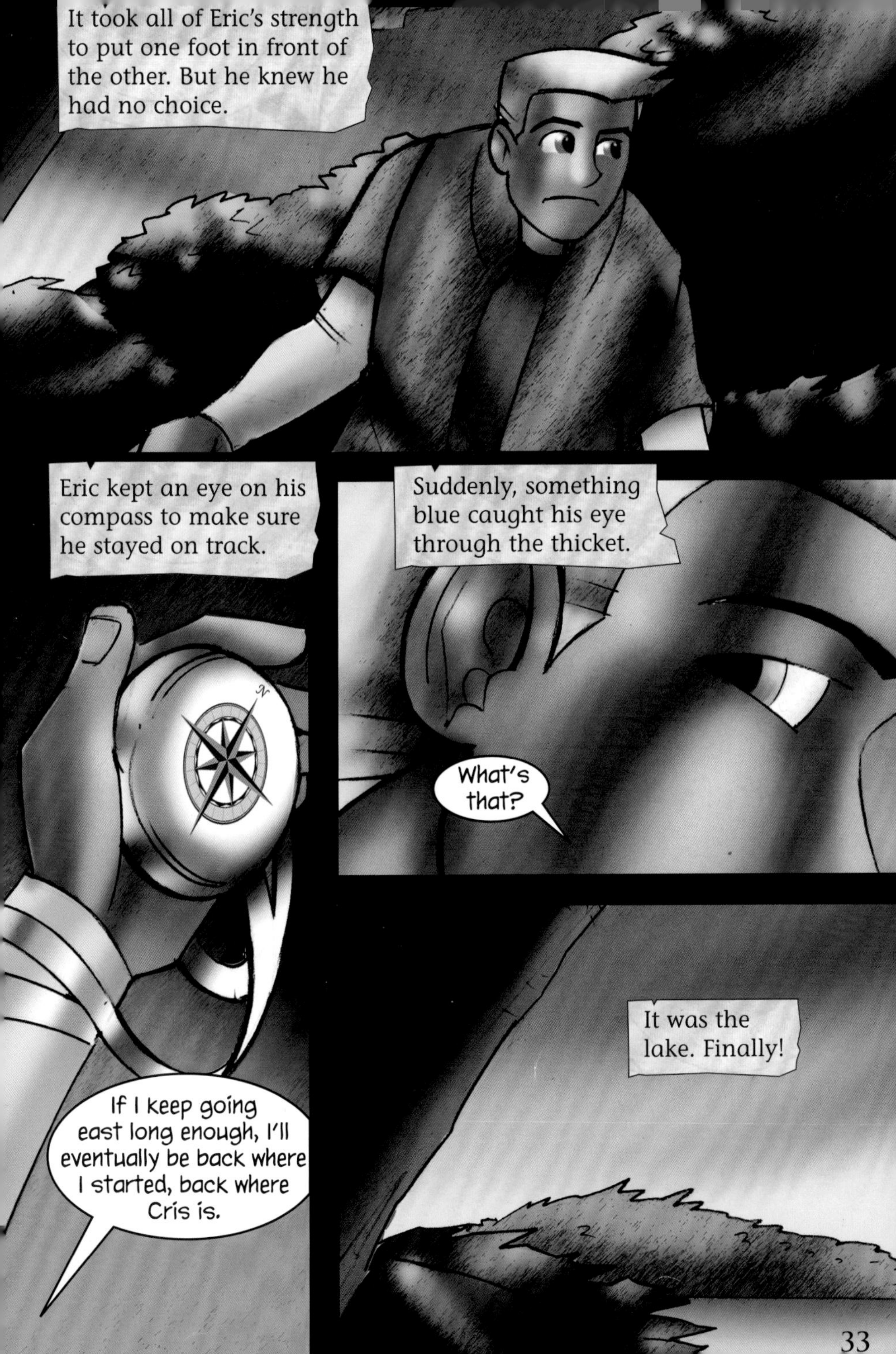
It took all of Eric's strength to put one foot in front of the other. But he knew he had no choice.
Eric kept an eye on his compass to make sure he stayed on track.
If I keep going east long enough, I'll eventually be back where I started, back where Cris is.
Suddenly, something blue caught his eye through the thicket.
What's that?
It was the lake. Finally!

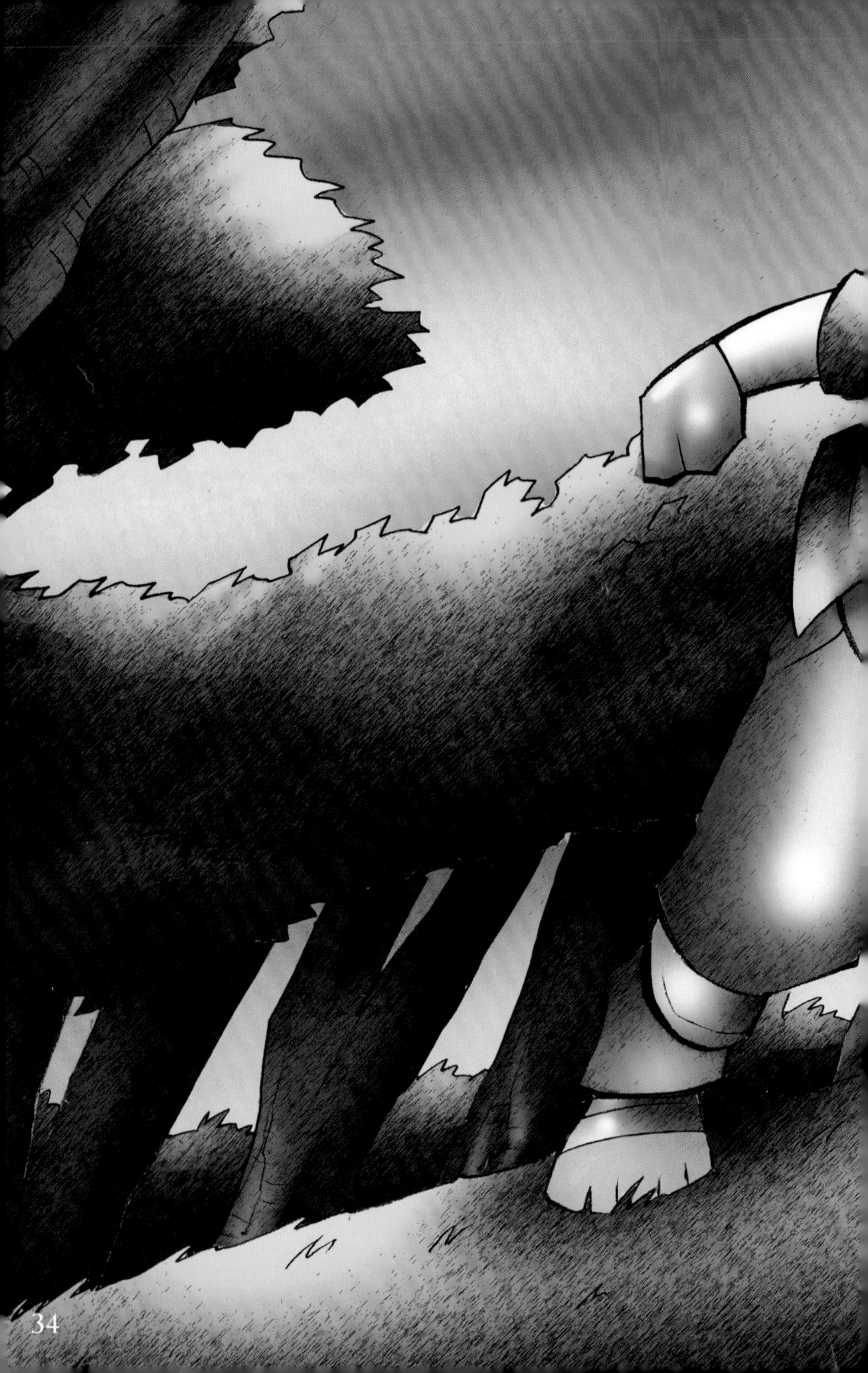

Yes! I must be close to camp!

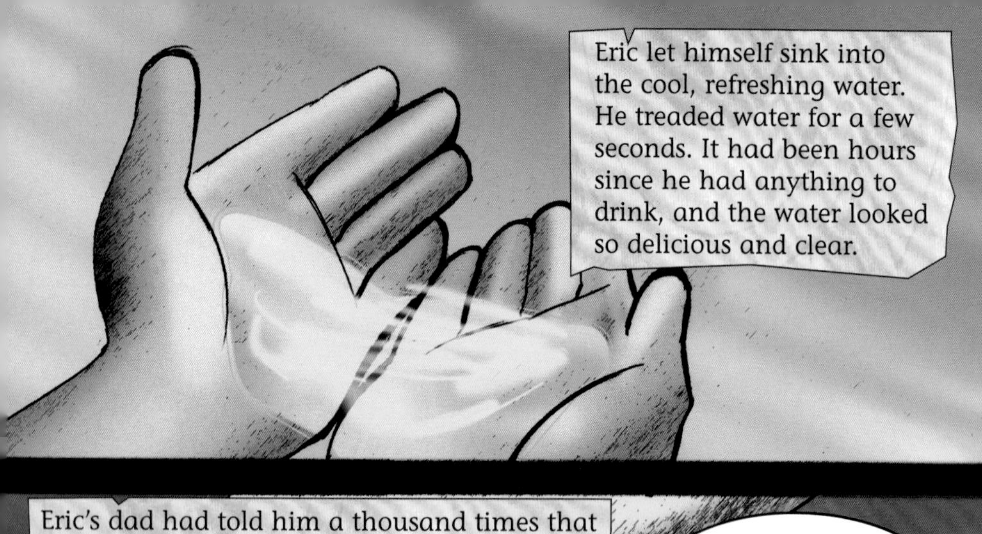

It was the best drink of water Eric had ever had. The cool liquid felt great going down his throat. The water was exactly what he needed. He kept drinking and drinking until his belly was full.

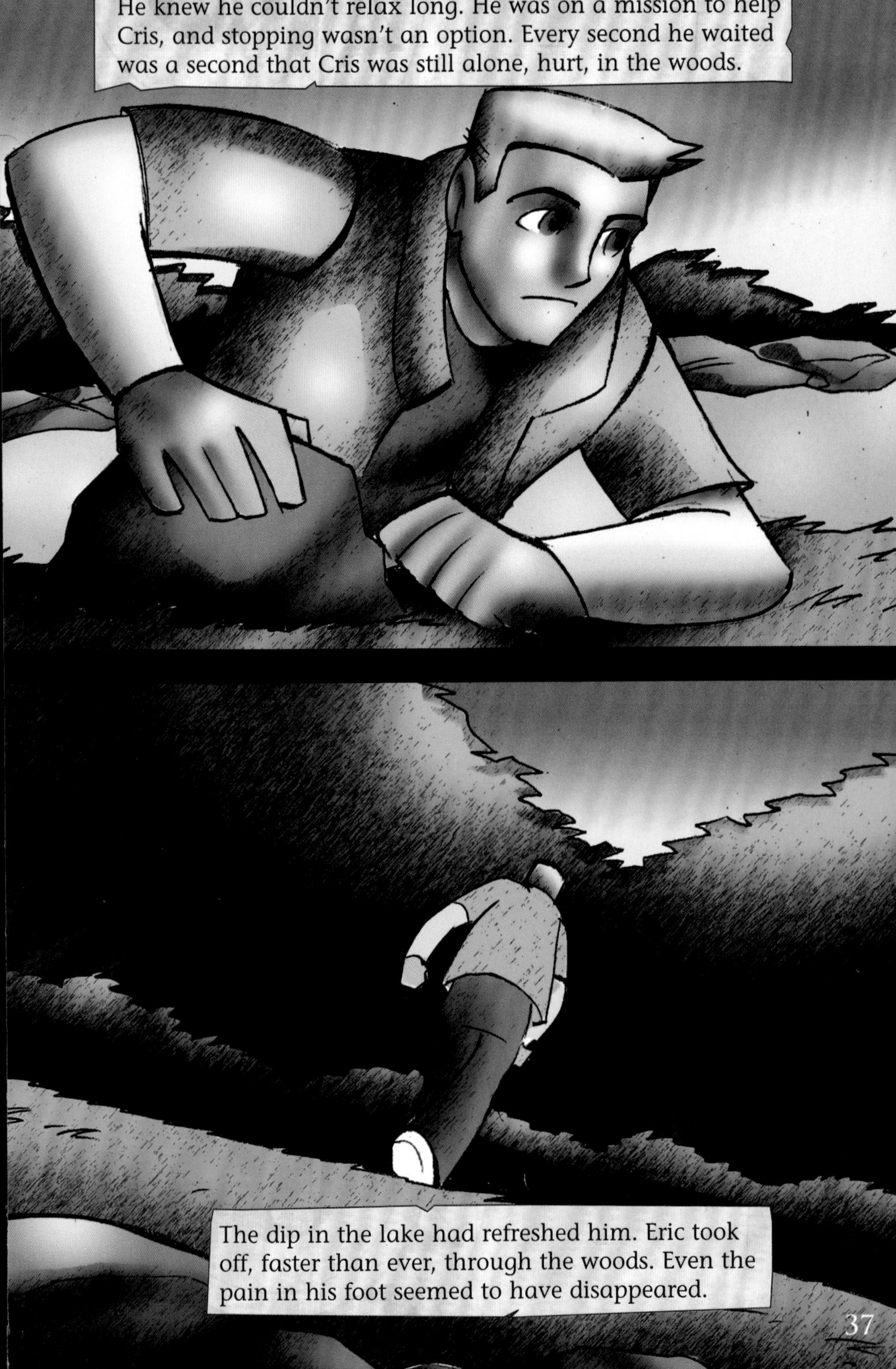
He knew he couldn't relax long. He was on a mission to help Cris, and stopping wasn't an option. Every second he waited was a second that Cris was still alone, hurt, in the woods.
The dip in the lake had refreshed him. Eric took off, faster than ever, through the woods. Even the pain in his foot seemed to have disappeared.

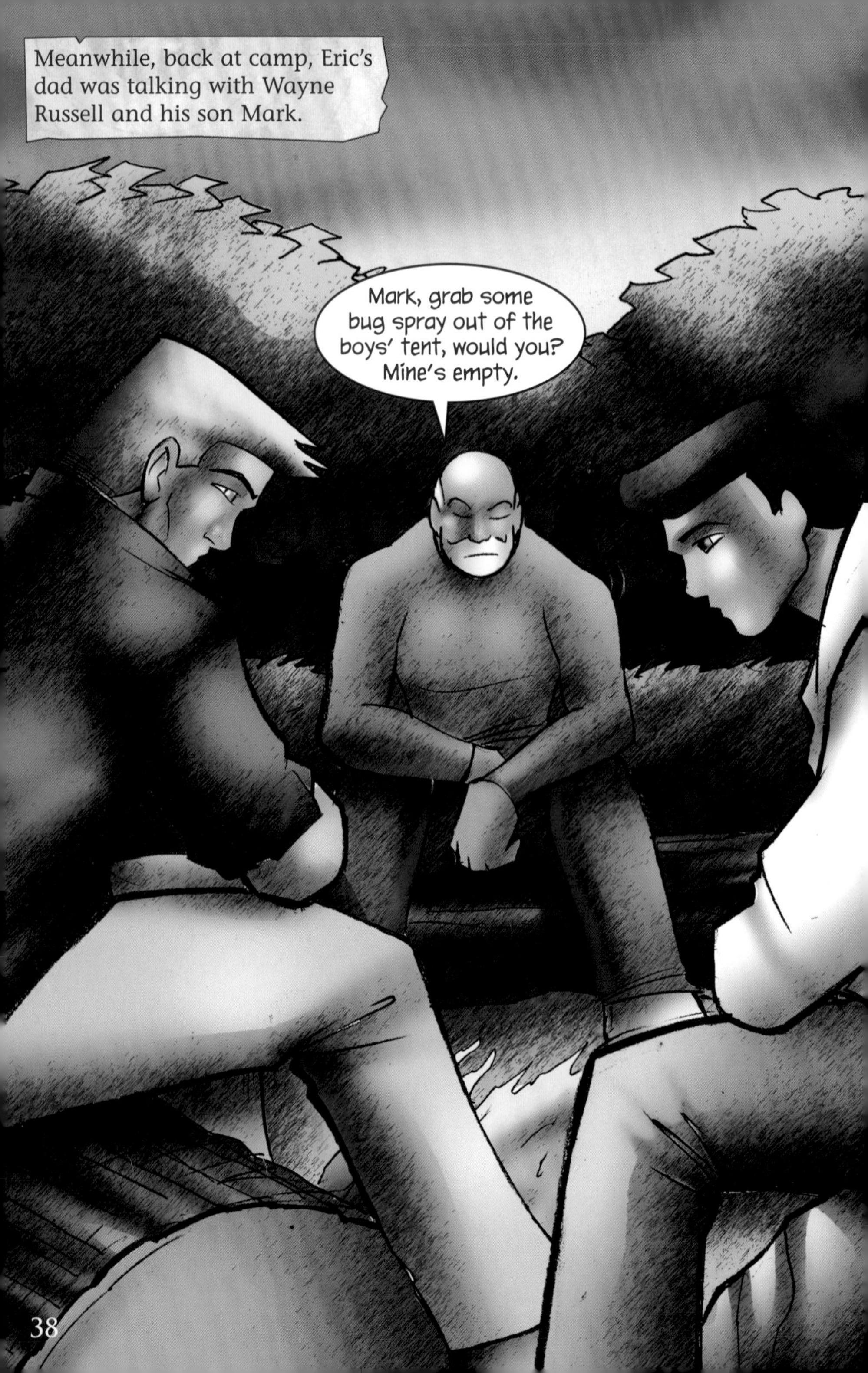

Meanwhile, back at camp, Eric's dad was talking with Wayne Russell and his son Mark.

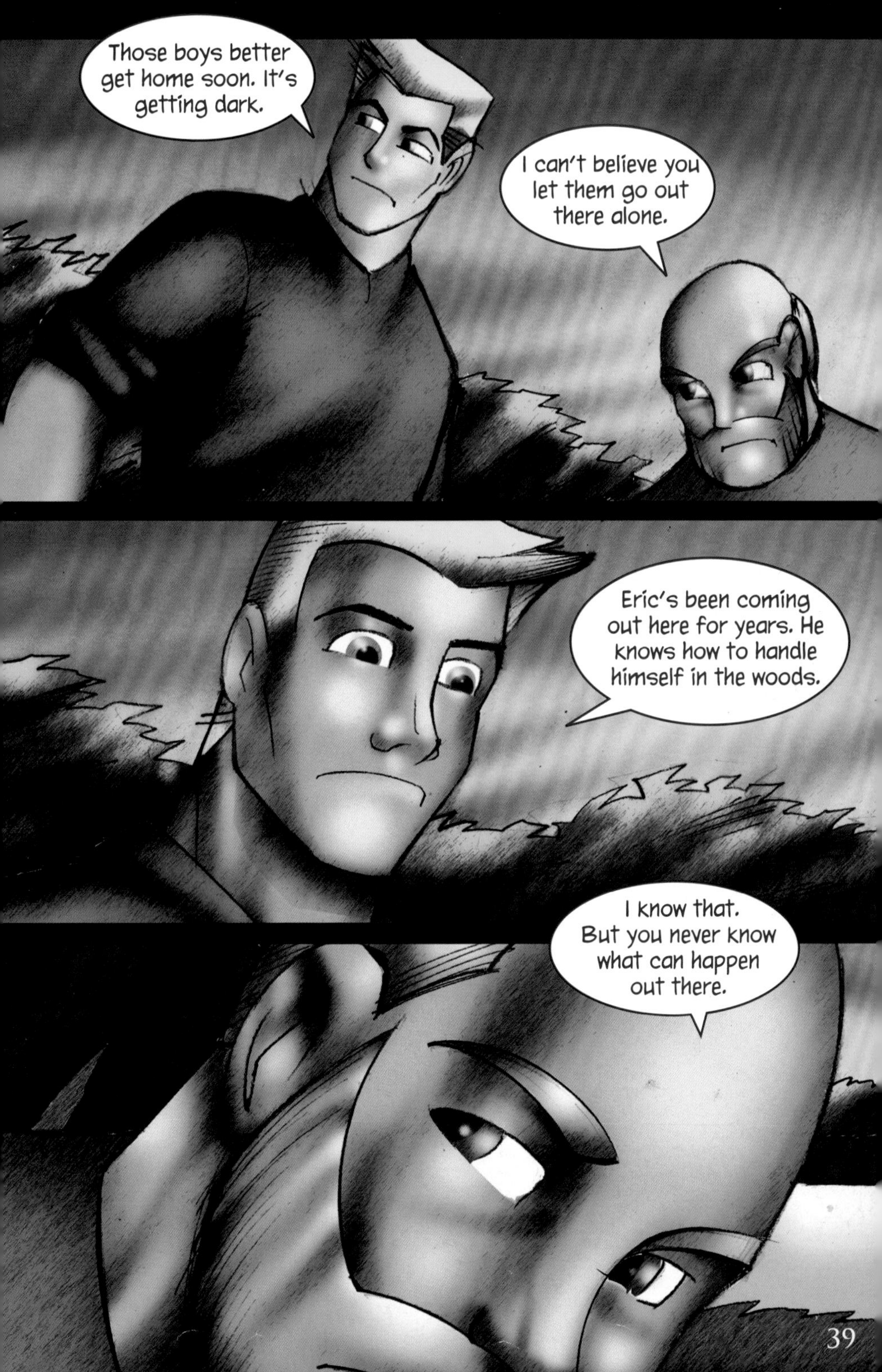
Those boys better get home soon. It's getting dark.
I can't believe you let them go out there alone.
Eric's been coming out here for years. He knows how to handle himself in the woods.
I know that. But you never know what can happen out there.

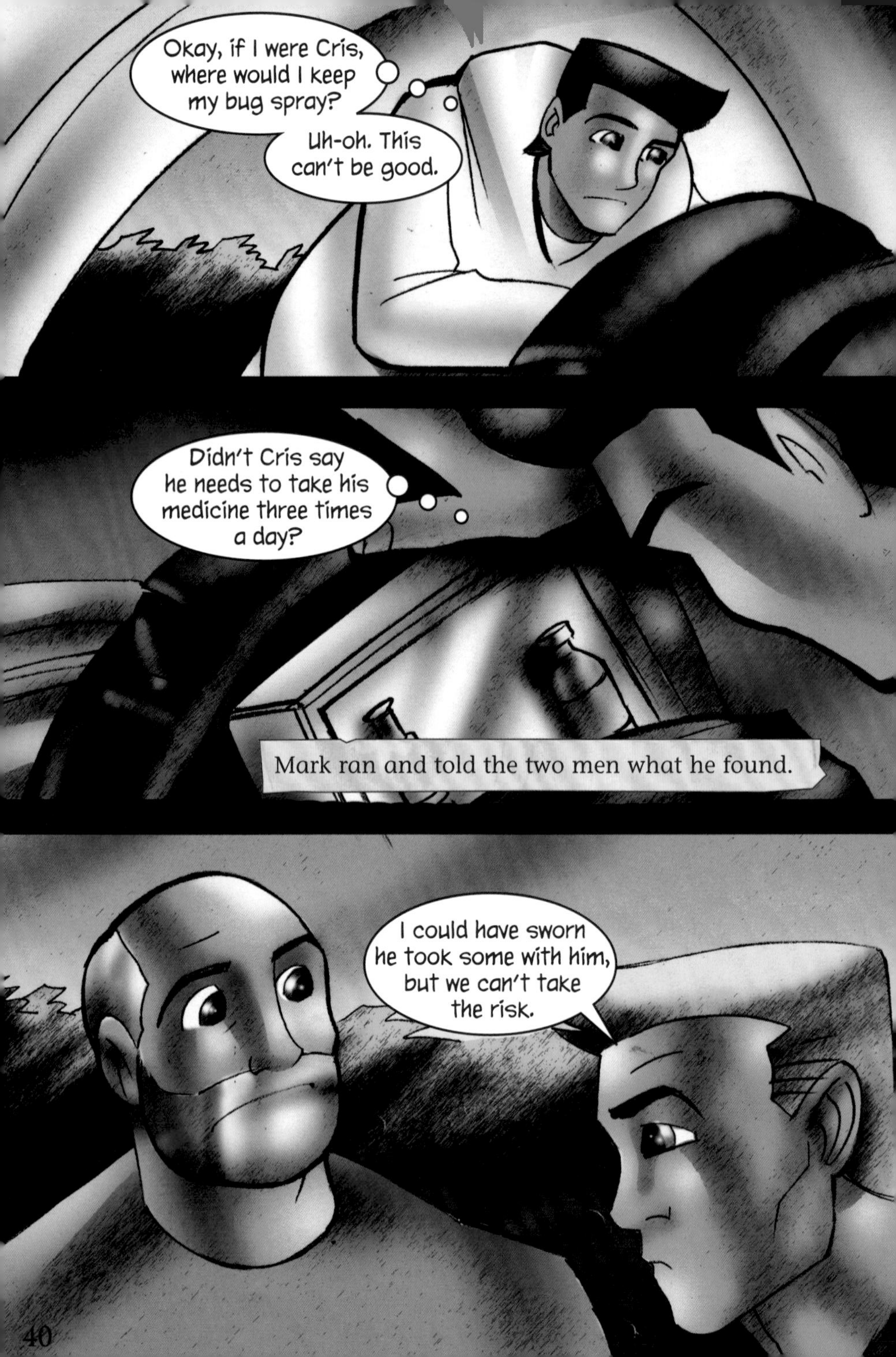
Okay, if I were Cris, where would I keep my bug spray?
Uh-oh. This can't be good.
Didn't Cris say he needs to take his medicine three times a day?
Mark ran and told the two men what he found.
I could have sworn he took some with him, but we can't take the risk.

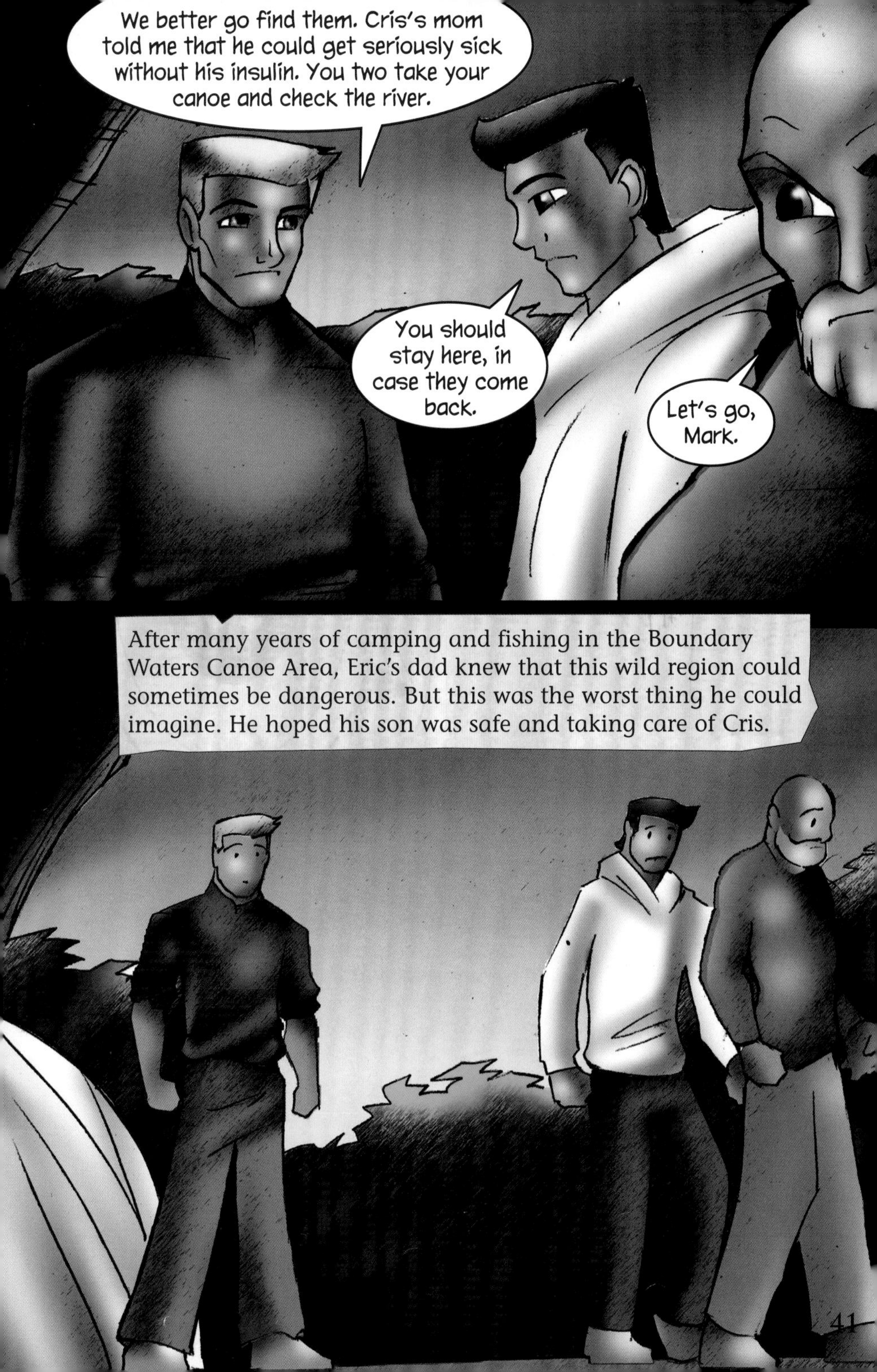
We better go find them. Cris's mom told me that he could get seriously sick without his insulin. You two take your canoe and check the river.
You should stay here, in case they come back.
Let's go, Mark.
After many years of camping and fishing in the Boundary Waters Canoe Area, Eric's dad knew that this wild region could sometimes be dangerous. But this was the worst thing he could imagine. He hoped his son was safe and taking care of Cris.

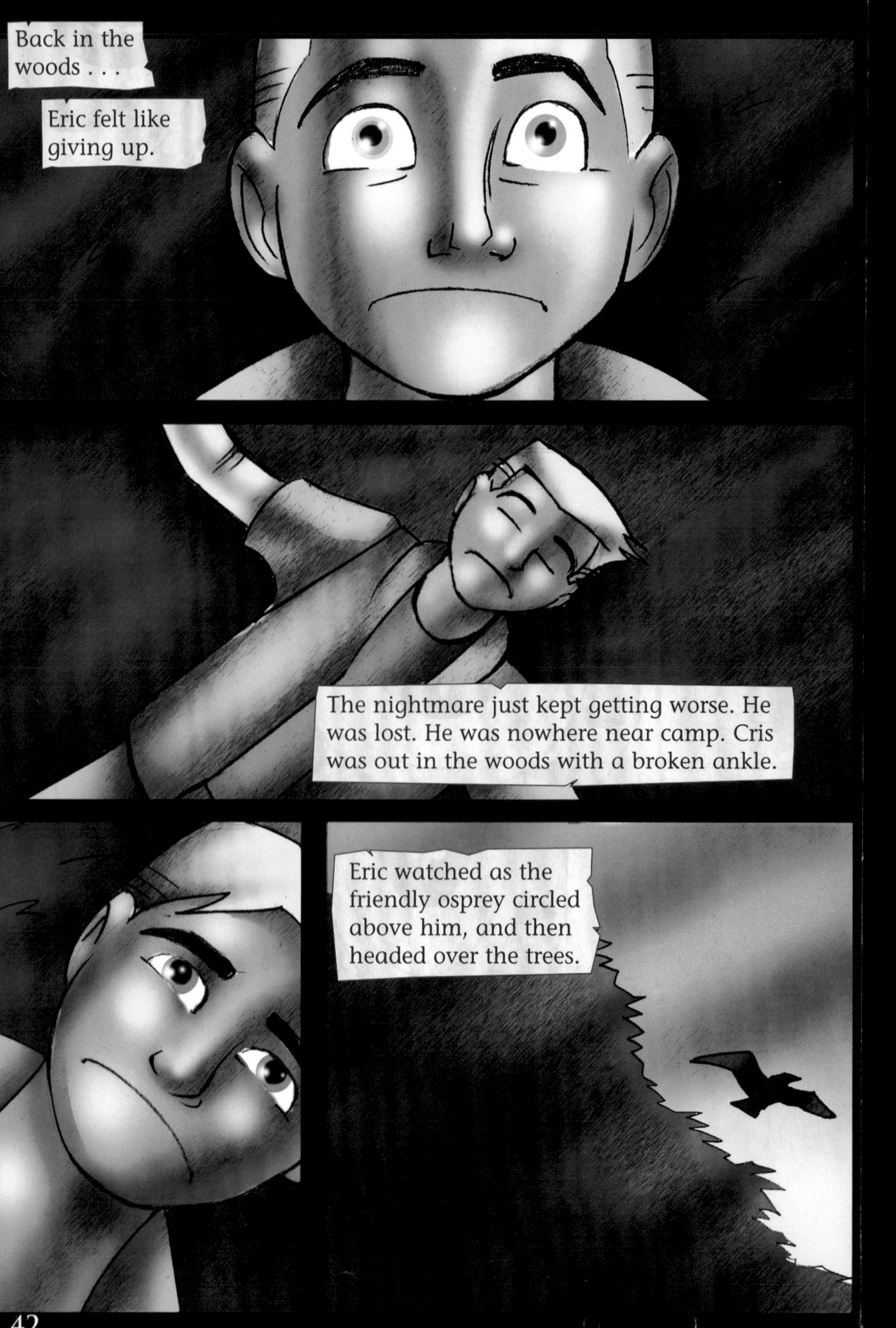
Back in the woods . . .
Eric felt like giving up.
The nightmare just kept getting worse. He was lost. He was nowhere near camp. Cris was out in the woods with a broken ankle.
Eric watched as the friendly osprey circled above him, and then headed over the trees.

Yes!
It was the portage trail! Used by canoers to travel between lakes, the portage trail would lead Eric to camp.
There's that bird again. Dad told me that ospreys are hunting birds. They eat fish. And fish are found in lakes and rivers.

CHAPTER FIVE

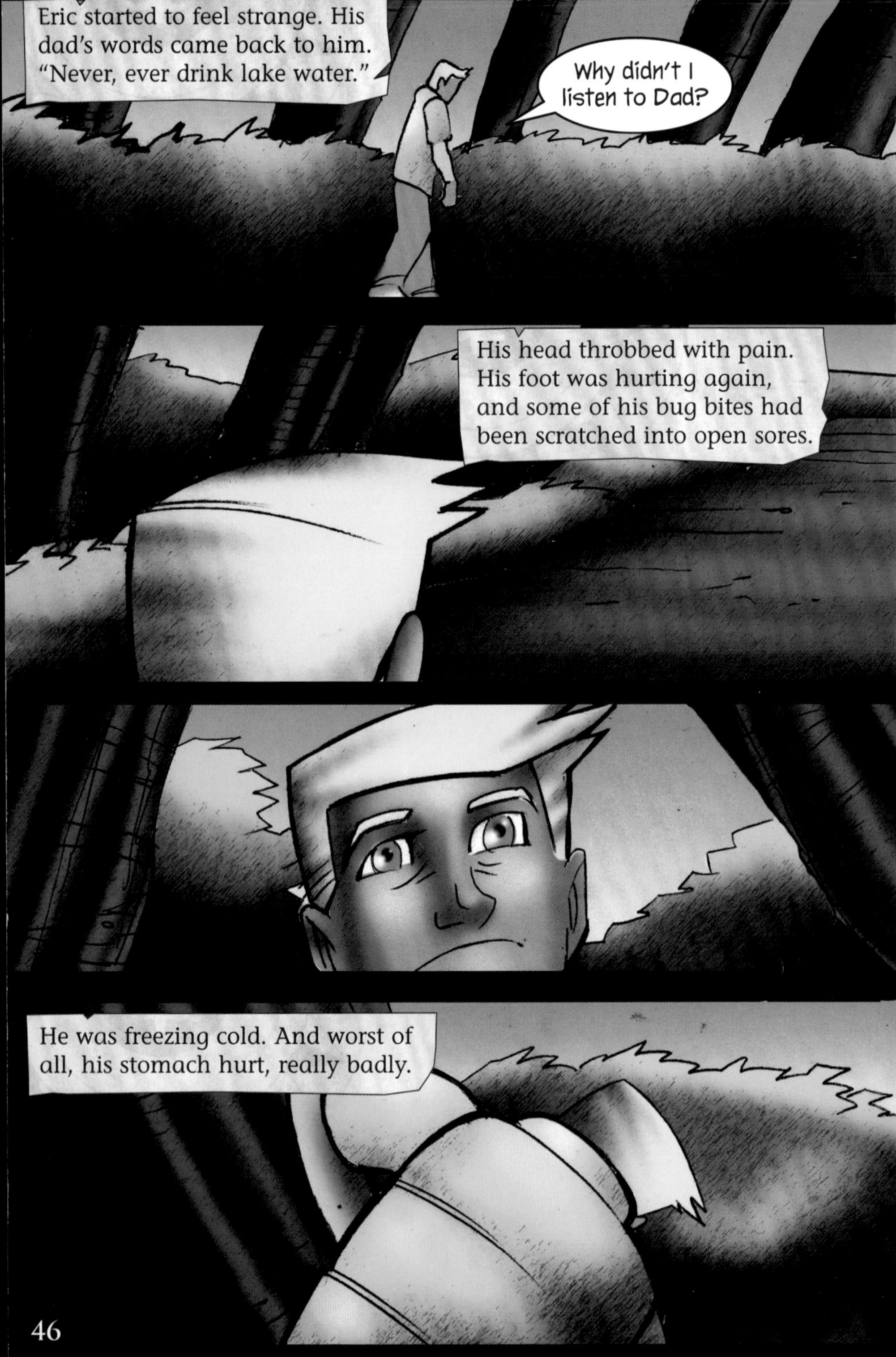
Eric started to feel strange. His dad's words came back to him. "Never, ever drink lake water."
Why didn't I listen to Dad?
His head throbbed with pain. His foot was hurting again, and some of his bug bites had been scratched into open sores.
He was freezing cold. And worst of all, his stomach hurt, really badly.

OHHHHHH!
A terrible pain shot through his body.

It's the lake water. "Never drink the lake water."
Like a poisonous snake, the pain crawled through his body.
Ugh.

If I ever get out of this alive, I promise I'll tell Dad he was right. I never should have drunk that stupid lake water.
Eric kept walking. But with each step, his stomach locked up more and more. It felt as if a knife was stabbing him!
The nightmare kept getting worse.

Eric collapsed. His legs wouldn't work anymore.

Help! Anybody!

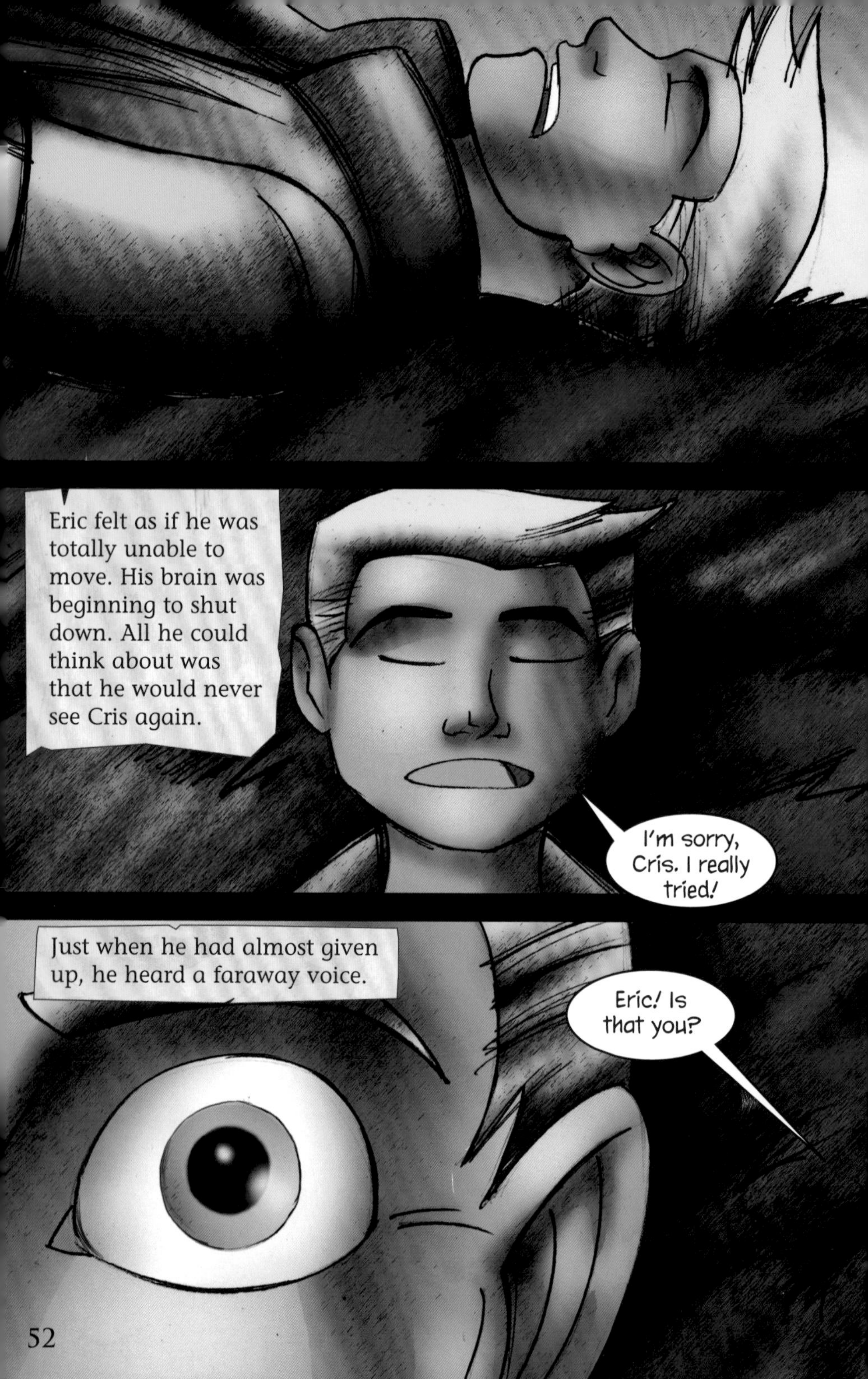
Eric felt as if he was totally unable to move. His brain was beginning to shut down. All he could think about was that he would never see Cris again.
I'm sorry, Cris. I really tried!
Just when he had almost given up, he heard a faraway voice.
Eric! Is that you?

CHAPTER SIX

OOOH!
In another part of the forest, Cris was sinking into serious trouble. He was thirsty, hungry, and without his insulin. And he didn't know where he was.

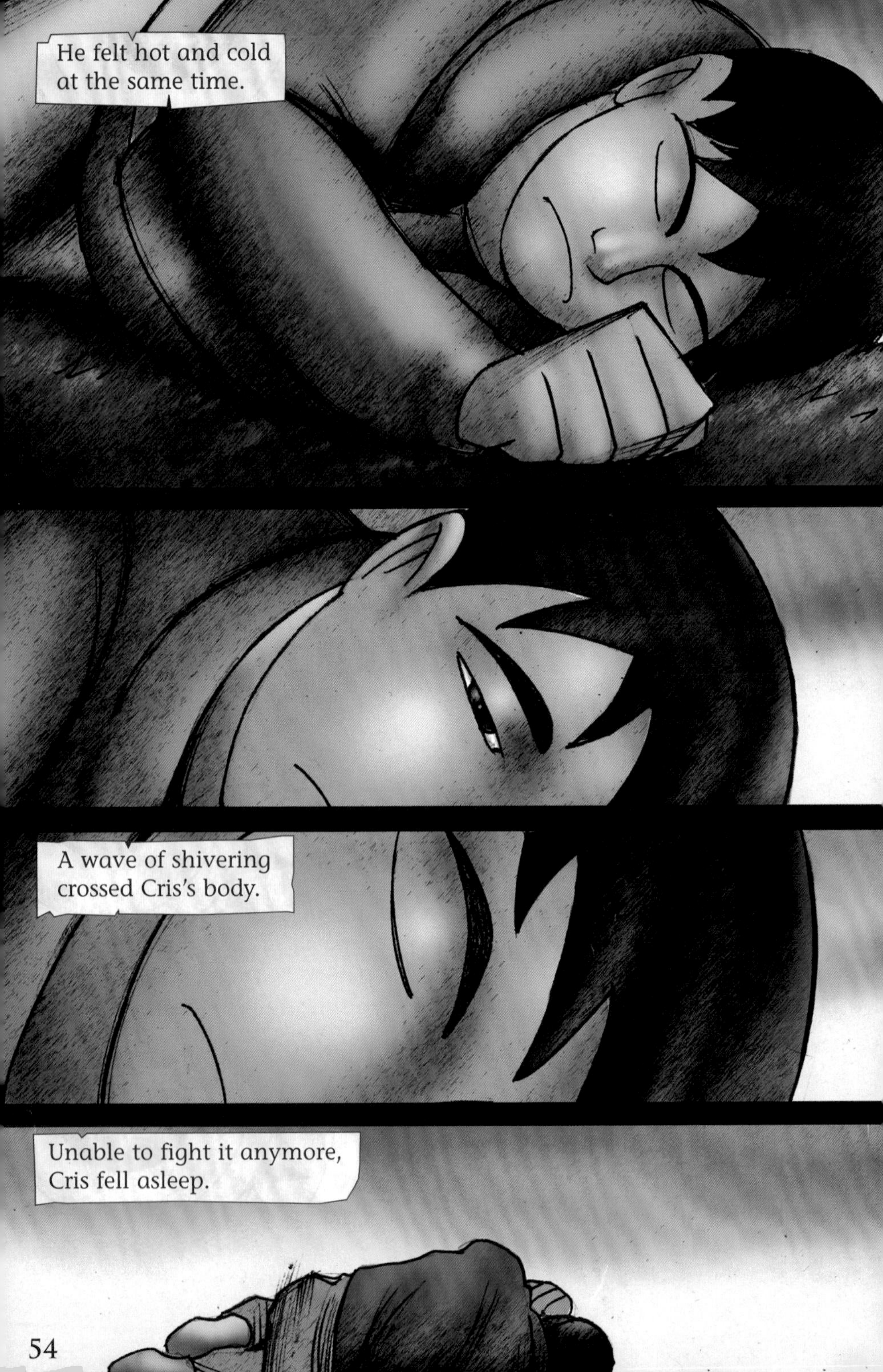
He felt hot and cold at the same time.
A wave of shivering crossed Cris's body.
Unable to fight it anymore, Cris fell asleep.

Meanwhile. . .
Eric!
Dad?
I'm by the river! Over here, Dad!

Hang on!
Only the river was between Eric and his dad.
I'm almost there, Eric!

Are you okay?
Yeah. I think so.
You're bleeding.
It's mostly mosquito bites. And my foot. I cut it on some rocks.
You're shivering, too.
I drank some lake water. It made me sick.
Lake water does that. Eric, I've told you a hundred times not to—
Dad, we have to get Cris!
I know. We found his medication in a bag, back at camp.
Dad, he's out in the woods alone, with a broken ankle!

He could go into shock without his medicine, Eric. How long has he been alone?
A few hours, I guess.
We better hurry.
Eric's legs were almost too weak to walk, so his dad helped him get back to camp. Eric couldn't believe how close he'd been. It had felt like he'd never make it.
The camp was empty when Eric and his dad arrived.
Where is everybody?
They're all looking for you.

I hope Cris is okay.
Here, drink some water.
Slowly.
Just a little sip.
The water hurt his throat going down, but right away, Eric felt better.

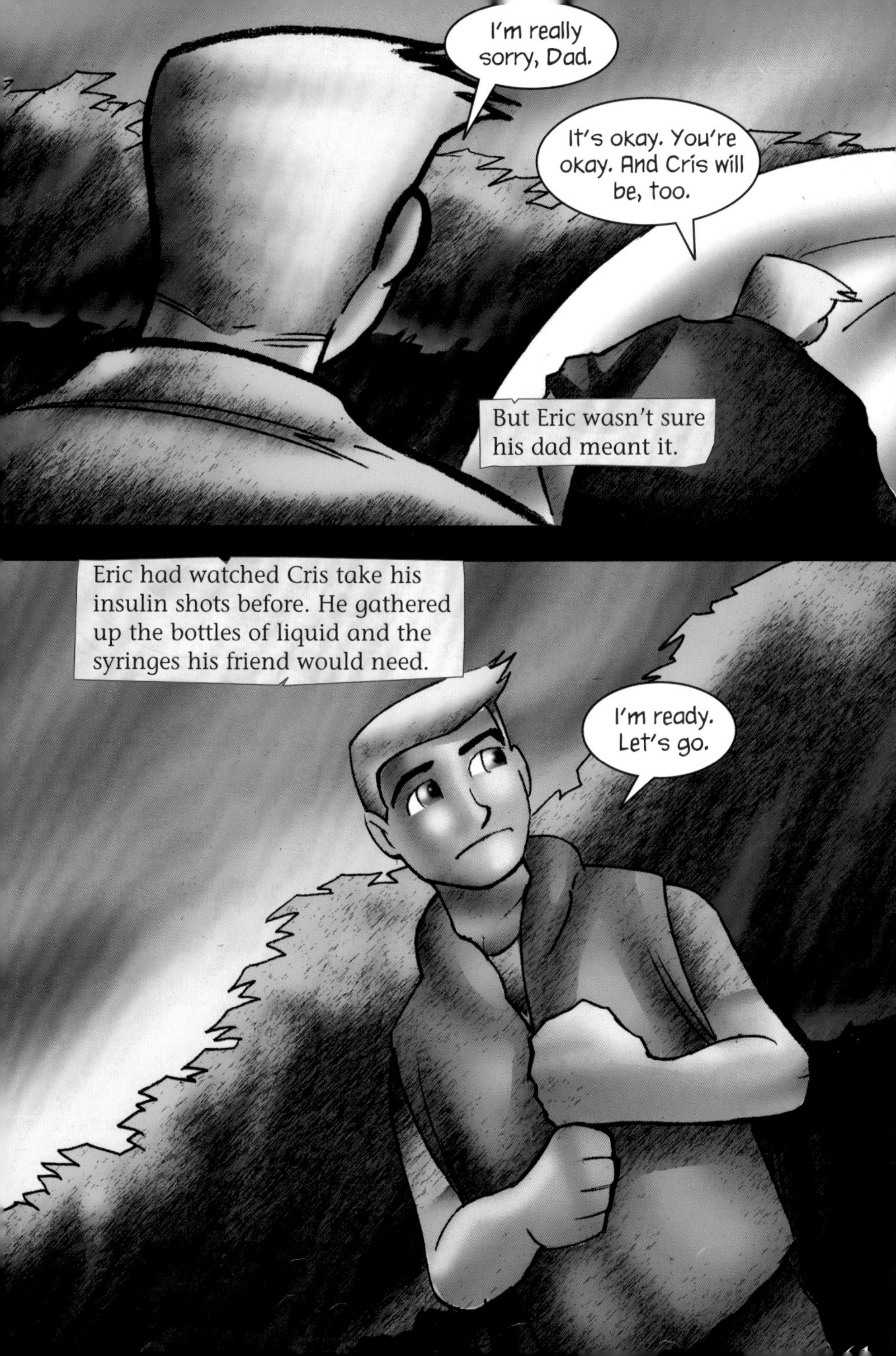
I'm really sorry, Dad.
It's okay. You're okay. And Cris will be, too.
But Eric wasn't sure his dad meant it.
Eric had watched Cris take his insulin shots before. He gathered up the bottles of liquid and the syringes his friend would need.
I'm ready. Let's go.

CHAPTER SEVEN

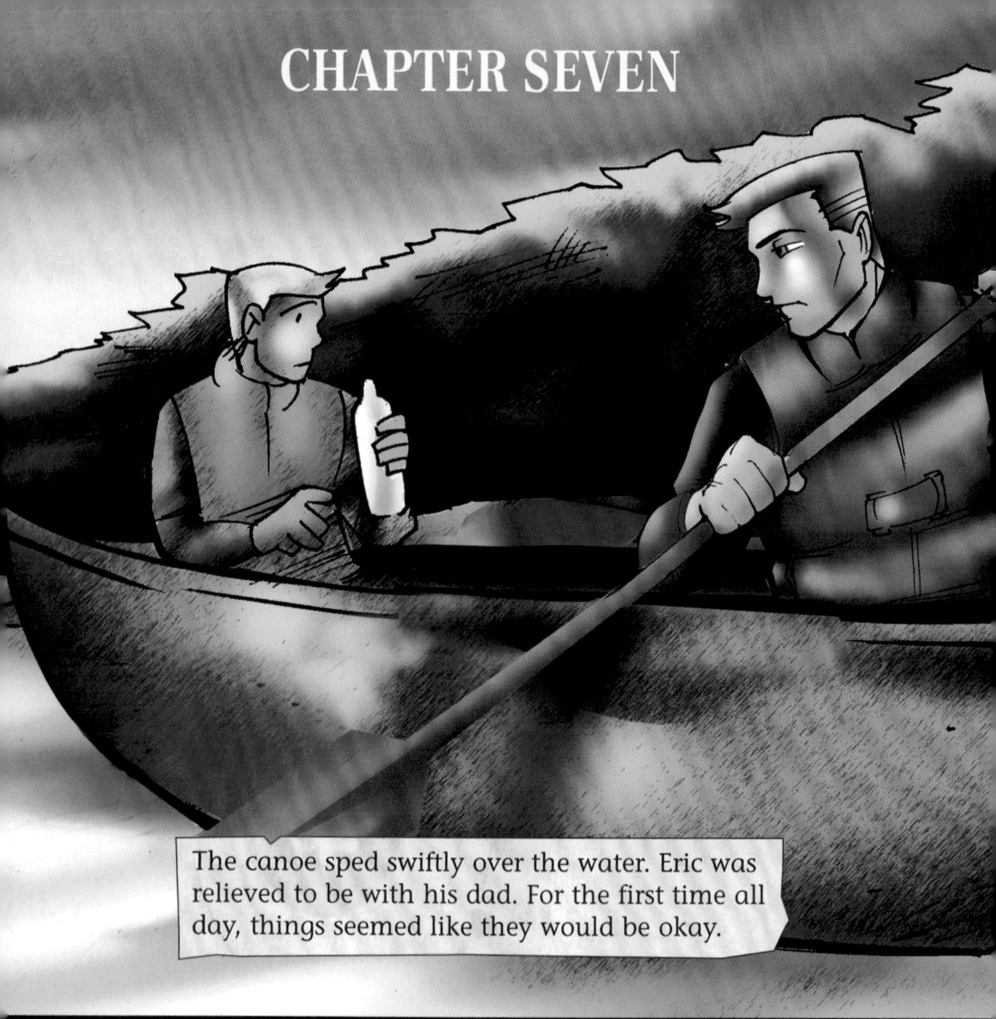

The canoe sped swiftly over the water. Eric was relieved to be with his dad. For the first time all day, things seemed like they would be okay.

Eric felt his stomach twisting into knots.
Suddenly, everything went fuzzy.
Eric!

Eric could barely see his dad leaning over him.
Eric? Eric, are you with me?
Slide back, Eric.
Eric's dad moved him into the middle of the canoe. The hard aluminum felt like a soft bed.
Hold on, Eric. I'm going to get you to shore.
Over here!

Russell, any sign of Cris?

They were at the Swift River.
We didn't find Cris.
But we did find his life jacket.

Eric didn't feel well enough to try to move from the canoe.
Eric said that Cris broke his ankle.
And he doesn't have his insulin.
He can't have gone far then. We'll find him.
Is Eric okay?
He drank too much lake water and threw up.

We better get moving.
Hold on.
There's a good chance we'll need to get Cris to a hospital.
No reception. I'll set off the smoke signals.
Mark remembered that they'd watched a video before entering the Boundary Waters. If there was an emergency, the video said, campers should light three separate smoke signals.
The smoke should get attention. They'll send in an emergency team.

Your dad and I will go and find Cris.
What about me? I have his medicine.
You stay here with Mark. You're too sick. We'll take Cris's medicine.
Eric didn't want to ask the terrifying question in his mind.
Dad, what if you can't find him?

We'll find him.
Okay. Good luck.
Mark and Eric went back to camp, where Mark quickly set up the smoke signals. And Eric, exhausted and still scared, finally managed to fall asleep.

Deep in the woods, Cris had never felt so alone. In the distance, he heard something moving through the trees. Could it be a bear? A wolf?

The animal sounds were coming closer.
Maybe if I lie here and don't move, whatever it is will go away!
The pain, the stress, and the fear all hit him at once. His body had been without food or water for hours. Cris passed out.

We need to give him his medicine . . . quickly!
He's unconscious. We'll have to carry him.
At least now he's safe.

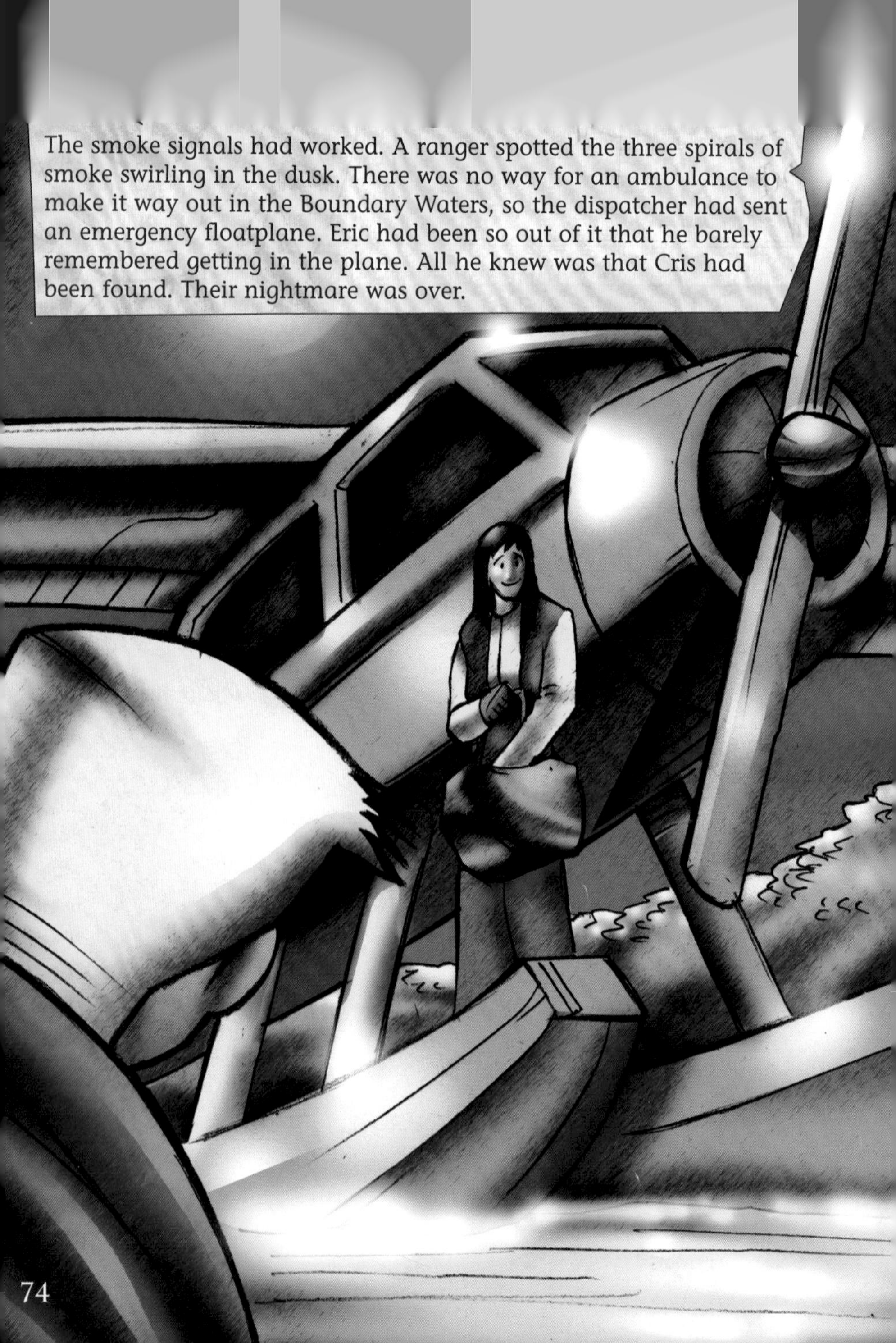
The smoke signals had worked. A ranger spotted the three spirals of smoke swirling in the dusk. There was no way for an ambulance to make it way out in the Boundary Waters, so the dispatcher had sent an emergency floatplane. Eric had been so out of it that he barely remembered getting in the plane. All he knew was that Cris had been found. Their nightmare was over.

You boys are lucky!
You mean we're lucky to be alive, right?
Yes. And lucky that your friends found you both before it got too dark!
Eric realized that Cris was still passed out. He wondered if his friend was in shock.
Is he going to be okay?

He'll be fine, once his core temperature gets back to normal and he gets some fluids in him.
His leg will need to be set and put in a cast, and we'll monitor both of you overnight at the hospital.
I'll meet you at the hospital as soon as I can, Eric. We just have to pack up camp and portage out of here.

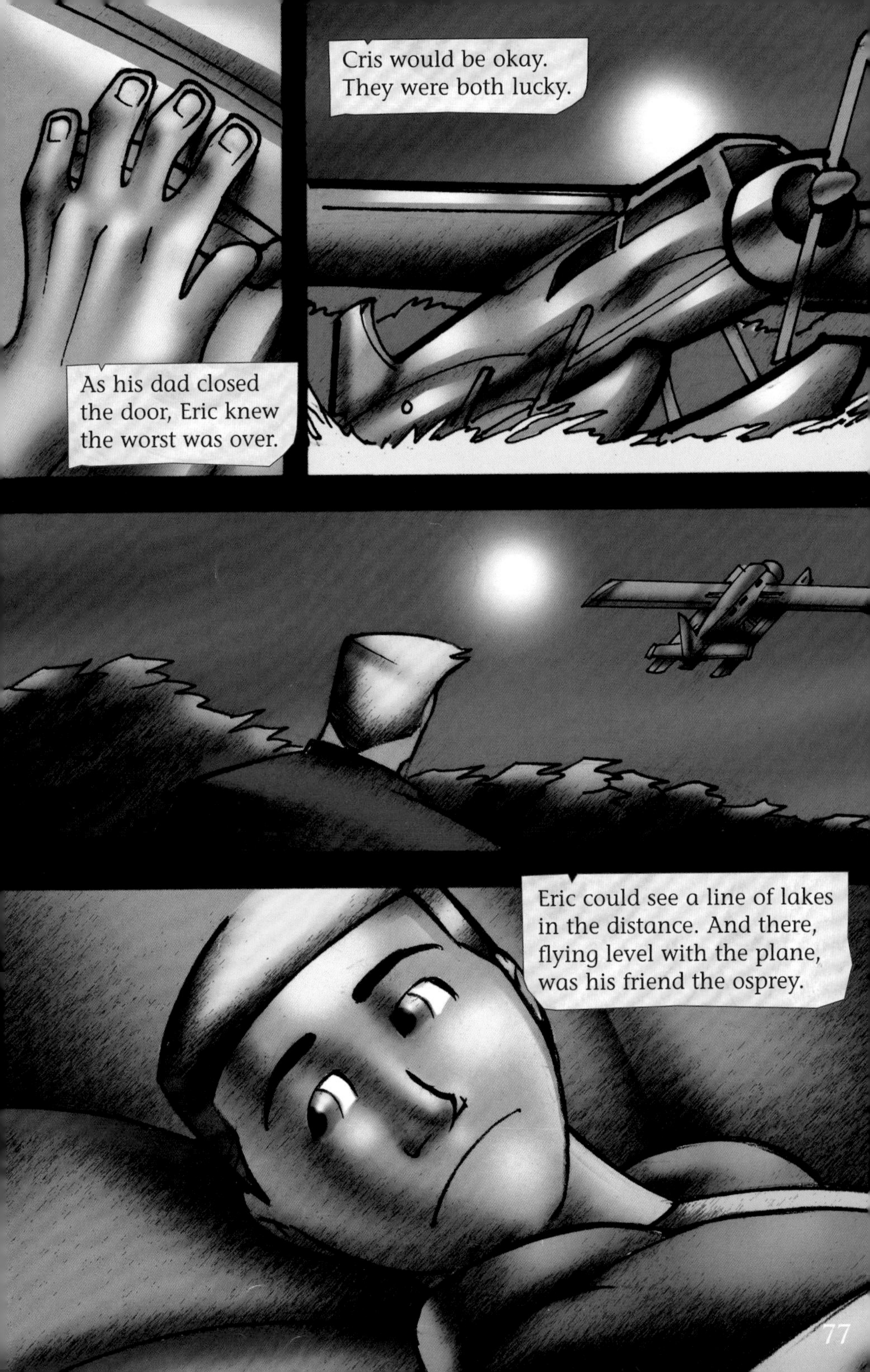
Cris would be okay. They were both lucky.
As his dad closed the door, Eric knew the worst was over.
Eric could see a line of lakes in the distance. And there, flying level with the plane, was his friend the osprey.

Below him was the white, shimmering water
of the Swift River. It looked beautiful again.
Calm and peaceful in the night.

See you next summer.

ABOUT THE BWCA

The Boundary Waters Canoe Area (BWCA) is part of the Superior National Forest, located in the northeast corner of Minnesota. Here are a few facts about this huge area:

At more than 1.3 million acres, the BWCA is the largest wilderness area east of the Rockies and north of the Florida Everglades.

About 200,000 people visit the BWCA every year to fish, hike, canoe, and enjoy the outdoors. In fact, it's the most popular wilderness area in the United States.

Although there is a large number of visitors, it's still easy to get lost. The BWCA has about 1,200 miles of canoe routes and 2,000 campsites.

The BWCA has about 1,775 lakes, and nearly all of them do not allow motorized boats. Visitors must hike or paddle their canoes to get from place to place.

Except for emergencies, airplanes are not allowed to fly below 4,000 feet while over the BWCA. The airspace above White House is the only other place in the country where flying that low is illegal.

Site of Eric and Cris's adventure.

United States of America

Minnesota

Boundary Waters Canoe Area (BWCA)

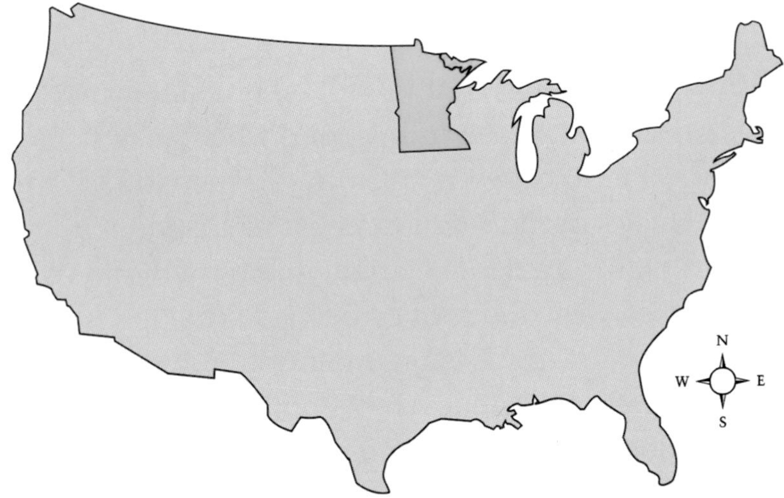

ABOUT THE AUTHOR

Chris Kreie grew up in the small Minnesota town of Princeton. As a kid, he played basketball, marched in the band, and took fishing trips with his dad to the Boundary Waters Canoe Area (BWCA). While exploring the BWCA, Kreie imagined all of the tales that could be told about this vast wilderness. He says, "Dramatic stories just ooze from a setting like that." Today, Kreie loves working as an elementary school librarian and spends his summers writing books like this.

ABOUT THE ILLUSTRATOR

Marcus Smith says that he started drawing when his mother put a pen in his hand when he was a baby. Smith grew up in Chicago, where he took classes at the world famous Art Institute. In Chicago he also designed band logos and tattoos! He moved west and studied at the Minneapolis College of Art and Design, majoring in both Illustration and Comic Art. As an artist, Smith was "influenced by the land of superheroes, fantasy, horror, and action," and he continues to work in the world of comics.

GLOSSARY

bacteria (bak-TEER-ee-uh)—microscopic living things that can sometimes cause disease

compass (KUM-pus)—a small device used for finding directions

diabetic (dye-uh-BET-ik)—a person who is diabetic has **diabetes** (dye-uh-BEET-iss), a disease where there is too much sugar in their blood

dusk (DUSK)—the dim time of day right before sunset

insulin (INN-suh-lin)—a chemical that makes sure you have the right amount of sugar in your blood. People with diabetes are given insulin.

osprey (OSS-pray)—a bird that hunts fish

portage (POR-tij)—a route on dry land that leads from one body of water to another

shoot the rapids (SHOOT thu RAP-idz)—to ride past dangerous rocks on a river while in a boat or canoe

thicket (THIK-it)—a thick group of trees or bushes

unconsciousness (KON-shuss-nis)—not awake or aware of your surroundings

upstream (UP-STREEM)—in the direction a river is coming from

DISCUSSION QUESTIONS

1. When Cris broke his ankle, Eric decided to leave him and search for camp. Do you think this was a good decision? Why or why not?

2. Eric's dad told him a thousand times not to drink the lake water. Why did he disobey his dad's warnings? What happened? Do you think he would make the same decision again?

3. People often learn from their mistakes. What mistakes did Eric and Cris make in the story? What could these mistakes teach them in the future?

WRITING PROMPTS

1. Every summer, Eric and his dad take a trip to the Boundary Waters Canoe Area. Write a story about a trip that you've taken with family or friends. What made your trip exciting?

2. When Cris's ankle is broken, Eric risks his life to help his friend. Pick one or two friends, and write about how they've helped you in the past.

3. Imagine that you were stranded in the wilderness and you could bring only three things. What three things would you bring and why?

ALSO PUBLISHED BY STONE ARCH BOOKS

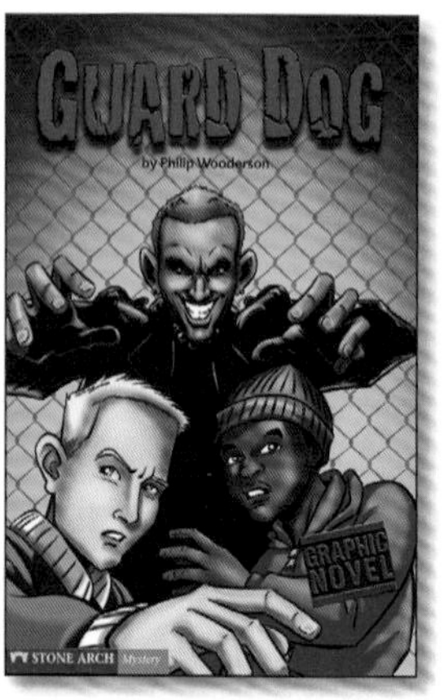

Guard Dog
by Philip Wooderson

Ryan would rather play his favorite video game Guard Dog than help his dad sell his artwork at the flea market. When the artwork is stolen, however, Ryan and his friend Steve take on the case. The two boys quickly learn that a detective's work is no game.

The Haunting of Julia
by Mary Hooper

Before Julia can blow out her birthday candles, the flames vanish into smoke! When she watches a replay on her dad's videotape, she sees a mysterious figure standing behind her shoulder. Julia suspects a ghost has blown out the candles and has come to haunt her.

Detective Files
by Steve Bowkett

Someone has stolen a priceless diamond from the city's museum! When police can't catch the crook, they call the world's most famous TV detective — Roy Kane.

Abracadabra
by Alex Gutteridge

Tom is about to come face-to-face with Charlotte, Becca's double. But there's something strange about this, because Charlotte died three hundred and fifty years ago.

INTERNET SITES

Do you want to know more about subjects related to this book? Or are you interested in learning about other topics? Then check out FactHound, a fun, easy way to find Internet sites.

Our investigative staff has already sniffed out great sites for you!

Here's how to use FactHound:

1. Visit *www.facthound.com*

2. Select your grade level.

3. To learn more about subjects related to this book, type in the book's ISBN number: **1598898280**.

4. Click the **Fetch It** button.

FactHound will fetch the best Internet sites for you.